For Bethan

Text and cover design by Louise Millar

Printed and bound in Belgium by Proost
for the publishers Piccadilly Press Ltd,
5 Castle Road, London NW1 8PR

1 3 5 7 9 10 8 6 4 2

A catalogue record for this book is available from the British Library

ISBNs: 1 85340 660 0 paperback
1 85340 655 4 hardback

*Jenny Graham lives in the Forest of Dean.
She has one daughter. A graduate of the Somerset College of Art,
Jenny has illustrated non-fiction books and advertising campaigns.
This is her first picture book.*

BILLY GOATS GRUFF

Jenny Graham

Piccadilly Press • London

Here are the three
Billy Goats Gruff.

Tiny Gruff,
Small Gruff
and Big Gruff.

They were very greedy goats and
ate up all the grass in their field.
Now they were hungry!

Big Gruff said, "We must cross
the bridge to find fresh, green grass."

But on the other side of the bridge
lived the bad, ugly troll!

But Tiny Gruff was brave.
He went first.
Trip trap! Trip trap!
across the bridge.

"Who's that?" cried
the troll. "I'm going
to gobble you up for
breakfast!"

"I'm too tiny for your breakfast," said Tiny Gruff. "Wait for my brother. He's much fatter!"

And the troll said,
"All right. But I can't wait all day!"

Small Gruff came next.
Trip trap! Trip trap!
across the bridge.

"Who's that?"
shouted the troll.
"I'm going to gobble
you up for dinner."

"I'm too small for your dinner,"
said Small Gruff.
"Wait for my brother. He's much fatter!"

And the troll said,
"All right. But I can't wait much longer."

Then along came Big Gruff.
Trip trap! Trip trap!
across the bridge.

"Who's that?"
roared the troll.
"I'm hungry! I'm going to
gobble you up NOW!"

But Big Gruff just said,
"Come and get me!"

So the troll jumped UP . . . .

But Big Gruff butted him
DOWN into the icy river.

The troll couldn't swim!
"Help me!" he cried.

The three Billy Goats felt very sorry
for the troll, so they pulled him out
of the water.

"Thank you, thank you!" said the troll. He was so happy that he told the Billy Goats Gruff that they could cross his bridge whenever they wanted to.

And strangely enough
they all became
great friends for ever!